Famous
Seaweed Soup

by Antoinette Truglio Martin

illustrated by
Nadine Bernard Westcott

Albert Whitman & Company • Morton Grove, Illinois

To my three little beach bums:
Sara, Hallie, and Robyn.   A.T.M.

To Becky and Wendy.   N.B.W.

Design by Karen A. Yops.
Text is set in Adroit Lite.
Illustrations are ink with watercolor.
Text © 1993 by Antoinette Truglio Martin.
Illustrations © 1993 by Nadine Bernard Westcott.
Published in 1993 by Albert Whitman & Company,
6340 Oakton Street, Morton Grove, Illinois 60053.
Published simultaneously in Canada
by General Publishing, Limited, Toronto.
All rights reserved. Printed in the USA.
10 9 8 7 6 5 4 3 2 1

Library of Congress Cataloging-in-Publication Data
Martin, Antoinette Truglio.
    Famous seaweed soup/Antoinette Truglio
Martin; illustrated by Nadine Bernard Westcott.
       p. cm.
    Summary: On a visit with her family to the
    shore, Sara gathers water, seaweed, snails,
    and smelly stuff to make her famous
    seaweed soup.
    ISBN 0-8075-2263-5
[1. Seashore—Fiction. 2. Soups—Fiction.]
I. Westcott, Nadine Bernard, ill. II. Title.
PZ7.M356764Fam 1993   92-31612
[E]—dc20   CIP
                                              AC

On a hot summer Sunday, Daddy laid out the blue-and-white striped beach blanket on the warm sand and set up the yellow umbrella for shade.

Mommy put Hallie on the blanket and searched for a rattle deep in the bottom of the green beach bag.

Hallie tasted her toes.

Sara dragged her red knapsack to the water's edge and dumped out everything. It was time to make her Famous Seaweed Soup.

"Who will help me get the water for my Famous Seaweed Soup?" asked Sara, grabbing her yellow pail.

"Not I," replied Daddy. "I'm on sunscreen patrol."

"Not I," replied Mommy. "I'm feeding Hallie her lunch."

"Umph, umph," replied Hallie through a mouthful of mushy sweet potatoes.

"All right," said Sara. "I'll do it myself."

And she did.

Sara waded out into the bay up to her knees where the water was cool and clear. Slowly, she turned around and around while carefully filling the yellow pail with only the top of the glistening bay. She carried the heavy pail of bay soup back to the beach and set it at the water's edge.

When the job was done, Sara asked, "Who will help me collect seaweed for my Famous Seaweed Soup?"

"Not I," replied Daddy. "I'm looking for our favorite radio station."

"Not I," replied Mommy. "I'm burping Hallie."

"Urp!" replied Hallie. "Ah goo."

"All right," said Sara. "I'll do it myself."
And she did.

Sara collected two types of seaweed. One kind was dry, brown, and crackly.

The other was wet, green, and slimy. She stuffed them into the yellow pail of bay soup that was waiting at the water's edge.

When the job was done, Sara asked, "Who will help me gather snails for my Famous Seaweed Soup?"

"Not I," replied Daddy. "I'm fixing the snarl in your reel so we can go fishing later."

"Not I," replied Mommy. "I'm chatting with my friend."

"Da da dee uh gaba gaboo," replied Hallie to *her* friend.

"All right," said Sara. "I'll do it myself." And she did.

Sara walked into the shallows of low tide where the snails were sunning themselves. Most were shy and small. The bigger ones slowly oozed their gooey bodies outside when Sara held them quietly in her hand. But they always popped back in when she tried to pet them.

"Don't worry," whispered Sara. "I'll bring you home after we're finished playing."

Sara gathered twenty-one snails. Seven had tiny barnacles on them, which are considered a delicacy by Famous Seaweed Soup lovers. She plooped the snails one by one into the yellow pail of seaweedy bay soup that was waiting at the water's edge.

When the job was done, Sara asked, "Who will help me comb the beach for smelly stuff?"

"Not I," replied Daddy. "I'm making the sandwiches for everyone."

"Not I," replied Mommy. "I'm washing sand out of Hallie's mouth."

"Blech! Blech!" replied Hallie through a mouthful of sand.

"All right," said Sara. "I'll do it myself."

And she did.

Sara skipped along and about
the beach and found a sandy
seagull feather, a smelly horseshoe
crab tail and two of its claws,
blue beach glass (a rare find!),

three shells with a bit of dried clam left inside, and a floppy see-through sand crab. She also picked up a dozen or so periwinkle shells for a necklace she was making.

Sara saved the seagull feather, periwinkles, and blue beach glass in her sundress pocket. She plopped the other smelly stuff into the yellow pail of seaweedy, snaily bay soup that was waiting at the water's edge.

When the job was done, Sara asked, "Who will help me stir in the sand for my Famous Seaweed Soup?"

"Not I," replied Daddy. "I'm teaching Hallie how to swim."

"Not I," replied Mommy. "I'm reading my book."

"Wee . . . gug gug," replied Hallie, splashing.

"All right," said Sara. "I'll do it myself."

And she did.

Sara carefully drizzled warm, golden sand into the yellow pail filled with smelly, seaweedy, snaily bay soup that was waiting at the water's edge. She stirred the soup with the seagull feather. She stirred and stirred until the seaweed soup was just right—famously right.

When the job was done, Sara said, "My Famous Seaweed Soup is ready!

"No one helped me get the water or collect the seaweed.

"No one helped me gather snails or comb the beach for smelly stuff."

"Oh," replied Daddy.

"Oh," replied Mommy.

"OO," replied Hallie.

"'Cause no one helped me," said Sara, "you will all have to eat my Famous Seaweed Soup!"

Daddy sloppily slurped. "Yum!"

Mommy daintily sipped. "Oh, wonderful. Much more flavor than yesterday's batch."

Hallie happily giggled. "Yeee!"

"Of course," said Sara. "It's my Famous Seaweed Soup—the best batch ever. And I made it myself!"